Christmas Escape

S L Davies

Published by S L Davies, 2022.

This is a work of fiction. Similarities to real people, places, or events are entirely coincidental.

CHRISTMAS ESCAPE

First edition. December 4, 2022.

Copyright © 2022 S L Davies.

ISBN: 979-8215123188

Written by S L Davies.

Chapter One

Peyton

The nurses said I was brave, the police said I was strong, what family I had left said that it was the right thing to do. But as I climbed off the plane in the middle of the tiny airstrip, on a blustering and snowy day that could only be described as bitter, I felt anything but strong and brave.

I'd never been to Alaska in my life. I never thought it was even a place that one day I would visit let alone consider living in. Out of sheer fear and probably a moment of insanity I opened a map that I'd asked the nurse to bring me and closed my eyes, simply pointing to a spot. When I opened my eyes, my finger was pressed on the name of Badger Valley, Alaska.

It didn't take much pressing for my father to purchase me a ticket and within the week I was on my way. A cast covered my left arm, while I still sported dark bruising under my eyes. It was the last time I would ever allow a man to lay a hand on me. I'd made excuse after excuse for Jason throughout our entire relationship. Every bruise I had a lie for. But when he came home drunk and rampaging through the house this final time, I thought I was going to die.

I closed my eyes and prayed that he'd make it a quick death. Instead, I woke up in hospital with tubes jutting out of my body. Four cracked ribs, a fractured eye socket and cheek bone. My nose broken and teeth knocked from the back of my mouth. My arm was shattered from where he'd stomped on me. My thighs had perfect boot print impressions.

The following days in the hospital were spent in a blur of pain medication, police visits, my mother crying into my dad's arms. The questioning of why? *Why didn't I tell them how bad it was? Why did I stay?* All the same questions I'd asked for years. But I couldn't answer their questions. I didn't have an answer for why I stayed. I would've said at one time that it was because I loved him. However, the more I thought about it, the more I knew that wasn't the truth. Jason was simply a nasty habit that I couldn't give up.

It was different now though. Here I was climbing down the steps carefully, hanging onto the railing and glancing out at the snow-covered surroundings of a tiny airport, not really more than an airstrip. Trees loomed in the distance; mountains surrounded the town. I was safe, I reminded myself as I stepped onto the tarmac and started towards the doors of the airport. Jason didn't know I was here. He wouldn't be able to find me. He'd been arrested and the prosecutor promised me that I wouldn't have to attend his trial. The police and prosecutor said my statement and list of injuries would be enough. I held onto hope that it was true. The thought of facing Jason again was a terrifying prospect.

I walked through the doors of the airport and felt my cheeks sting as the warmth of the building touched my frozen skin. Plastic chairs sat on top of blue worn carpet. An old laminate desk took up one wall of the room. A large man rugged up began to bring in bags of luggage from beneath the plane. I didn't have much. Only one suitcase that Mom had purchased me and a few clothes to get me through.

Dad organized me a room at a bed and breakfast lodge simply called Badger Valley lodge. Dad had chuckled commenting about the unoriginal name. But I was too lost to even think about it. Everything was moving so fast. I spotted my red suitcase and headed towards it. Plucking my suitcase out of the neatly stacked pile, I turned and tried to clear my mind so that I could work out where I needed to go next.

I couldn't remember if Dad had said there were cabs or uber here. I went towards the reception desk to enquire when I heard my name being called. Looking over my shoulder a tall man with long blonde hair and the brightest blue eyes I'd ever seen stood with a broad smile. He waved his hand at me and started to step forward. I glanced around, expecting him to be here for someone else. Which made no sense since I'd clearly heard him call my name.

"Yes," I replied with a slight frown of confusion.

"Hi, I'm Micah," he introduced himself with a grin that in other circumstances might have been quite infectious. The way that he introduced himself it was as if I was supposed to know who he was. The name sounded familiar, but I couldn't place where from. "Sorry, I'm Micah Howards. I own Badger Valley lodge. Your dad contacted me and told me you were flying in today. I offered to give you a lift."

I sighed out a long breath and gave him a weak smile, nodding my head. "Thank you. I've been on a lot of pain medication, so couldn't remember what my dad told me."

Micah chuckled and shook his head. "No problem. Is that your only suitcase?" he asked pointing at the red case that I held in my unplastered hand.

I looked down at the case. I'd forgotten it was even there. Sudden shame engulfed me as Jason's voice rang through my mind at how stupid I was. Tears started to burn at the back of my eyes. I glanced quickly back up at Micah. He frowned and then widened his eyes.

"Hey, hey, it's okay. You are safe here," he tried to assure me.

I swiped at the stray tears that had managed to slip from my eyes and smiled a wobbly smile. "Sorry," I apologized. "I'm a bit overwhelmed."

"It's alright. Your dad gave me a brief explanation as to what has brought you to Badger Valley. I promise though, that we are a great little town, and everyone is friendly and welcoming. There is nothing to worry about here," Micah said as he took my case from my hand and turned beginning to lead me out of the building and towards the waiting town.

I sucked in a deep breath. I hoped that he was right. I hoped that I had no more worries. I just couldn't be quite as optimistic as Micah was. Not yet anyway.

Chapter Two

Micah

When Joseph, Peyton's father contacted me to book a place for his daughter to stay, he'd warned me that she'd had the shit beat out of her. But nothing could've prepared me for the sight of Peyton. Her right eye was still swollen. Bruising dripped down her cheeks and she had distinct fingerprints on her neck.

Peyton's arm was in a cast that went up over her elbow and held in a sling. She looked frazzled and I couldn't blame her in the least bit. The bastard that did this to her had a lot to answer for. Anger bubbled in the pit of my stomach as I thought about what kind of man could do something like that to a woman he was supposed to love.

I shook my head to wipe the heavy clouds that were threatening to engulf me. I watched my mother every day until my father finally succeeded in killing her. Once I was old enough to get out of the foster system and make it on my own, I'd worked every job I could find. Finally saving enough to buy the lodge. Now, I kept at least two rooms available for women just like Peyton.

I wouldn't charge her for the room. She could stay there for as long as she needed. Peyton was as safe as she could be at the lodge. Badger Valley was one of those towns, where everyone knew everyone. So, if her ex-husband were to miraculously find her and come chasing after her, he would stand out and word would race around.

I lifted the trunk of my car and slipped Peyton's simple suitcase in the back. When I glanced over at Peyton, she stood shivering with her arms folded across her chest. Alaskan winters were notorious. They were freezing. Snow coated everything and the wind blew through you, cooling your core temperature in minutes.

"Come on, jump in the car and that will warm you up," I said with a bright smile as I opened the passenger door.

Peyton nodded her head and gave me a brief smile. It was forced. She wasn't just trembling because of the cold. She was also scared. I couldn't blame her. This must be the most overwhelming thing she'd probably ever faced..

I jogged around the front of the car and slipped into the driver's seat. As soon as I brought the engine to life, I cranked the heater to fill the car with warm air. Peyton's cheeks and nose was pink as she leaned forward and put her fingers in front of the vent, warming them up.

"Do you have warmer clothes?" I asked.

Peyton glanced over at me and shrugged her shoulders. "Mom and Dad bought me a jacket and some thermals but I'm not sure it is going to quite be enough," she admitted.

I nodded my head. No one could imagine the bitter cold of Alaska until they got here. "We will organize you some warm clothes to get you through."

Peyton's brows pulled into a frown, and she shook her head. "I'm not a charity case," she said so quietly that if it wasn't for the silence of the car, I wouldn't have heard her. There was venom in her voice. My eyes widened as I realized that I'd put my foot in it. I'd never meant to make her feel like I was treating her like charity.

"I'm sorry, that's not how I meant it," I apologized quietly as I watched her. She faced the front of the car and didn't make eye contact with me. When I reached out to turn her face to look at me, I quickly dropped my hand when she recoiled and pressed herself tightly against the passenger door.

Peyton let out a shaky breath and when she glanced over at me, I noticed the tears that clung to her lashes. I sighed to try and swallow the anger I was feeling. It wasn't anger that was aimed at Peyton, but at her ex-husband. This girl was nothing more than a scared little rabbit.

"I promise you Peyton that I don't mean to treat you as a charity case. I just want to help and take some of the pressure off you," I explained.

Peyton's shoulders relaxed and she slowly exhaled before looking over at me. "I'm sorry," she whispered. "I didn't mean to snap at you. I appreciate that you are trying to help me."

I smiled at her and nodded my head. "I can only imagine how overwhelming this is for you. And if you need me to back off, then please tell me. I don't want to encroach on you. I want you to feel safe here."

Peyton nodded and gave me another forced smile but didn't say anything. I turned my attention to the road, flipping on the indicator before pulling away from the curb and heading back towards the tiny village of Badger Valley. I prayed that Peyton would find her healing, just as I had.

Chapter Three

Peyton

I wasn't a complete stranger to snow. It snowed where I grew up. But nothing would have prepared me for the sheer amount of it in Alaska. Trees were ladened with it drooping their branches down to the ground. When the sunshine caught on a freshly fallen snowflake it twinkled as if winking. It was beautiful. I stared out the window wordlessly as Micah drove from the airport to the lodge that I would call home for the time being.

I didn't know what I was going to do I had to get work. I couldn't rely on Micah to keep me fed, clothed, and housed. Especially since I snapped at him that I wasn't a charity case. Mom and Dad helped me to set up a bank account and they put in a few thousand dollars that would get me started. But the sooner I was able to find some work the better.

I had no idea if there were jobs even available in Badger Valley. The truth was I didn't know a single thing about the place. For all I knew it held the lodge and that was it. I continued to watch the window as the forests of snow-covered pines slowly began to change into homes. The homes quickly became a row of businesses. A bakery, diner, and bar. I was shocked, the town appeared to be a lot bigger than I'd anticipated.

It was still a tiny town in comparison to where I'd come from. But I guess I hadn't even expected there to be anything more than the lodge let alone a school and a large town hall. Christmas lights were strung along the light poles and red and green Christmas decorations covered the whole town.

"Everyone in Badger Valley gets together every year and decorates for Christmas. We often have tourists who come for the skiing," Micah explained as I took in the main street of Badger Valley.

"It's beautiful," I murmured quietly.

Micah chuckled. "It sure is. You've chosen a great little place to start again in."

"Is it safe?" I asked wondering honestly if I would be hidden from Jason in such a small town. All of the questions I should've stupidly asked before I moved here. It was just another one to add to the list of where Jason was right. *He always said I was stupid. I guess he was right.* I moved away from everyone and everything I knew, without even first checking to see if it was a viable place to hide.

"Peyton, you are well protected here. Everyone knows everyone. The cop in town Brody, is a good guy, he keeps a keen eye on things. If anyone comes here that doesn't appear to fit in, they will know. You're safe here."

I sighed. This was going to take time to get used to. *I was free.* Yet I still felt like I was held captive by Jason. He always said that if I ever left him, he would kill me. I believed every word of what he said. I knew that him being held in jail and then charged for his assault on me was going to piss him off further. He wasn't going to let it go.

I hoped he would. I hoped that it would be enough to make him give up on me. But my gut told me I was going to be looking over my shoulder for a long time. And no matter how good Brody the cop was, if Jason wanted me dead, he would find a way to make it happen. I just had to make the best out of this chance while I had it. I felt so morbid thinking about my fate, and I wondered when it happened that I accepted my death so easily.

I didn't say anything else as Micah drove to the end of the main road and turned into a large driveway. The lodge wasn't some small quaint little building. It loomed over the street. Easily the largest building in Badger Valley. But for as big as it was, the building was beautiful. It looked old and had a lot of character. Almost as if it were actually alive. I could almost sense it breathing in the essence of every person that had crossed the threshold.

Micah killed the engine and glanced over at me. He was a handsome guy. If I'd met him before I met Jason, I definitely would've been interested. His blonde hair hung in natural waves around his shoulders. His blue eyes were almost the colour of the clearest ocean. And when he smiled it lit up his entire face.

A knock on my window startled me and I spun to see the biggest animal I'd ever seen. A moose with enormous antlers was staring into the window. A gasp got caught in my throat as I peered out at the beast.

"Micah," I whispered.

Micah chuckled. "That's Maurice. He is Badger Valley's resident moose. He won't hurt you. He is just a bit of a peeping tom and likes to see what is going on."

Micah opened the driver's door while I still sat staring out at the enormous beast that was watching us through the passenger window.

"Here you go Maurice, I bought you a pastry," Micah said as he reached into the back seat and pulled out a paper bag. I watched in astonishment as the moose basically skipped around the car towards Micah. I could have sworn the moose smiled as Micah pulled out the sticky bun from the bag.

Maurice the moose took the bun from Micah's hand in one bite and swallowed it down. Bellowing out a happy call, Maurice smooshed his nose against Micah's chest before walking down the driveway and into the town.

I sat in the passenger seat in shock. I wasn't sure what to think. I'd never seen a moose in the wild. Let alone one that almost appeared human and ate sticky buns.

"Let's get you inside, it's too cold out here," Micah called, shaking me out of my shock. I opened the passenger door and followed him up the stairs to the front door of the lodge. *My home. For now.* But at least it was a small piece of safety.

Chapter Four

Micah

Peyton followed me into the lodge in silence. I had a feeling it was going to take her a long time before she trusted anyone again, let alone another man. From what her father had told me her ex-husband beat the hell out of her during their entire marriage. Now that she was free, she didn't know what to do with that freedom. It was going to take time. And I refused to push her too fast.

"This place is beautiful," Peyton said quietly.

I turned around in the foyer to take her in. She looked tiny in the large foyer. I noticed it at the airport, Peyton appeared to crumple into herself. She had perfected a stance that made her nearly invisible. I looked forward to the day that she was able to stop hiding and stand up straight with her chin lifted high.

"It *is* beautiful. Bessy was built in 1856. One of the first building's in Badger Valley. I think the church was the first," I explained. Peyton looked at me with genuine interest on her face.

"Bessy, you have a name for the building?" Peyton asked.

I chuckled and nodded my head. "Yep, as soon as I stepped into the lodge it was like she whispered her name. I've called her Bessy ever since."

"You talk about her like she is living and breathing."

I laughed and shrugged my shoulders. "Sometimes I think she is. You will notice soon enough. She is very protective of the people who come to live here."

Peyton stared at me as if scrutinizing what I was saying. It was true, sometimes I could have sworn that old house was a living, breathing entity. When I was growing up, the stories were that the place was haunted. We all thought it was a witches manor. When I got the chance to buy a place, I knew the only building in Badger Valley I wanted, was Bessy.

I'd called in one evening, close to dark and just looked up at Bessy. There was something about her that continued to call me. It was solidified in my mind. *She was to be mine.* After that things just seemed to happen. The previous owner put a for sale sign out the front the following day. He accepted my short settlement and even accepted the amount I offered without argument. At the end of the day Bessy was meant to be mine.

I'd walked in the front door the day I got the keys and it almost felt like she embraced me. I made a promise in that moment that I would care for her and be selective on who came through her door. Bessy helped that. Often if people that I didn't trust tried to enter, the door would lock. She even had a habit of tripping people up who she didn't like. I trusted Bessy's opinion on a person.

It seemed that Bessy liked Peyton, as she stayed completely silent. A scent rose from the kitchen of freshly baked bread. A scent I'd grown used to smelling when the house liked someone here.

"Are you baking?" Peyton asked.

I shook my head. "No, Bessy likes that smell," I replied with a shrug of my shoulder.

Peyton looked at me like I'd lost my mind. I guess I could be considered completely bat shit crazy. I let my home decide who I liked and who I didn't. But I didn't care what other's thought. Bessy hadn't steered me wrong yet.

"Come and I'll show you your room," I said with a smile.

Peyton nodded and silently followed behind me. I saw out the corner of my eye as she looked around the house and gently caressed her fingers along the dark wood of the staircase. I smiled inwardly. Peyton loved Bessy and in turn I knew that Bessy would protect Peyton. I gave Bessy's wall a gentle pat in thanks and heard the pipes gurgle in response. It was like she was reassuring me that she was going to care for Peyton. It was the best I could ask for.

I walked to the end of the hall and one of the large main rooms that I kept specifically for women who were escaping domestic violence. I pulled the key from my pocket and opened the door, waving Peyton in. I made sure to stand back and not crowd her as she glanced around the room.

"This is a beautiful room," she said.

With a smile I nodded towards the door that came off the bedroom. "There is a bathroom in there, that has a big bath and shower. The windows open and you can control the radiator here if it isn't warm enough. The wardrobe should be able to hold everything. If you need anything though, make sure you tell me."

Peyton stopped looking around the room and glanced over at me. Her eyes were filled with tears. She opened and closed her mouth as she tried to find what she wanted to say.

"I'm safe now," she said almost as if she was trying to reassure herself.

I smiled and nodded. "You are safe now."

"When am I going to feel it?" she asked.

I sighed and shrugged my shoulders. "Every woman is different. Some feel it straight away, other's take longer. You take as long as you need to get your bearings. No one is going to judge you for healing at your own pace."

What I didn't tell her is that some women never felt safe. Sometimes for some women it was too hard for them to face freedom. They were the women that broke my heart as I watched them go back to their abuser. That was my mother. There until the day my father killed her. I cleared my throat and forced a smile to my lips.

"I'll let you get settled. I'm going to be in the kitchen preparing dinner, there are a few people staying here," I explained.

Peyton smiled and nodded her head. "Do you need help to prepare dinner?"

My smile was more genuine when I answered her. "Not tonight. But maybe if you feel up to helping me make meals tomorrow that would be good."

Peyton nodded emphatically. "I'd like that."

I returned her smile and turned to leave the room allowing her to settle into her new home. Shutting the door behind me I whispered a quiet word to Bessy about looking out for Peyton. Something in my gut told me she was going to need more care than others.

Chapter Five

P eyton
I felt like I'd walked into an alternate universe. A moose that ate baked goods and liked to visit the human residents of Badger Valley. As well as a house that had a name and a personality.

"I hope you like me Bessy," I whispered. I didn't think I could handle it if the house hated me too. The pipes gurgled, startling me. I shook my head and chuckled at the ridiculousness of the situation. There I was talking to a house like she was a living and breathing being.

I placed my suitcase on top of the bed and started to unpack my meagre possessions. Mom had insisted on buying me some clothes as all of my stuff was back at the house, I'd lived in with Jason. I couldn't stand the thought of going back there. So, it wasn't hard to let Mom buy me new clothes. Enough to get through until I could find some work and earn the money to buy more.

Once my clothes were packed away, I stepped into the large bathroom. The bath looked enticing. For my entire marriage, Jason had dictated when and what I could do. At first, he'd sold it to me that he was an alpha, a Dom and I was his submissive. When I first started dating him, I looked into the BDSM relationships, and it appealed to me. However, it soon morphed, and I realized that this was no longer in the realms of a healthy Dom/Sub relationship. Jason was just an abusive asshole.

I shook my head as I tried to shake the memories out of my mind. It was going to take a long time before I would get over what he did to me. And I thought it was going to take even longer to ever trust another man again. Reaching over to the taps on the bath I twisted them and watched as the bath filled with steaming water.

Wishing I had some bubble bath I shucked my clothes off and dipped my toe in the hot water. Hissing at the sudden warmth on my cold toes. Once my foot was submerged it slowly got used to the heat and I was able to step completely into the bath before sitting down carefully so as not to get my cast wet.

I leaned my head back against the tub and closed my eyes, sighing out a long breath. I couldn't remember the last time I was absolutely free. It was well before I met Jason. I would have only been a teenager. I'd spent a lot of time in the hospital thinking about what this new freedom would be like. I was able to take a bath whenever I wanted. I could go to bed when I was tired, rather than having a set bedtime. I could eat whatever I liked and not worry about the calories. It all sounded fabulous. But it terrified me at the same time.

Jason's rules and abuse was so deeply ingrained in my system I feared that my mind wasn't going to allow me to break free. On the last day I was in hospital one of the nurses brought in a cream bun for me. The guilt that I felt eating it, made me sick and I could only take a few bites of the sweet pastry. Even though the taste of it had filled my mouth with pleasure. It was such a confusing situation to be in.

I wondered if other women went through the same thing. *Or was I simply crazy that I wasn't able to embrace my freedom with both hands?* Sighing again I carefully dunked my head under the water and allowed the warmth to soak through my hair to my scalp.

By the time the water was cold, I'd managed to think myself into a stomachache. I dried myself off, feeling the exhaustion that I seemed to carry everywhere with me wash over. Yawning I slipped into the yoga pants and sweater that Mom had got me. I glanced at the bed trying to decide whether I should take a nap or go down to the kitchen to help Micah.

Even that decision was a dilemma. I felt like I owed Micah a lot. After all, from what Dad had told me, he was opening this room for me rent free until I healed and got on my feet. He didn't put a time limit on how long that would be. But at the same time, my body was still healing.

I glanced between the door and the bed unable to decide what I needed more. My guilt and the need to pay back Micah was strong, but my body was screaming at me that it needed sleep. Finally, I decided to head towards Micah. However, it seemed that Bessy had other ideas.

I twisted the knob on the door to find it locked tight. I knew that Micah hadn't locked the door behind him because the key was still sitting on the dresser beside the door. I twisted at the lock again, and it refused to budge. I tugged on the door once more with a frown pulling at my brow. But no matter what way I turned the knob the door refused to budge. Surprisingly I didn't feel any sense of panic about being stuck inside the bedroom. That didn't make any sense. I should have been screaming and clawing at the wood of the door. Instead, something inside me told me I was safe, and this was Bessy's way of making me rest.

"Bessy, do you want me to sleep?" I asked in exasperation. As if in answer the damned house groaned.

I shook my head and rested my forehead against the warm wood of the door. "I'm going mad. I'm now listening to a house." I said with a huff. I gave the doorknob one more twist, realizing it was still locked. I turned and pulled the blankets back on the bed.

Slipping in under the blankets, warmth cocooned me. I felt even safer. With my head cushioned on the pillows and the weight of the blankets surrounding me, I felt like I was being held in a warm embrace.

"Thanks Bessy," I whispered as I closed my eyes and allowed sleep to take over. I could have sworn as I fell into a dreamless sleep, I heard the door unlock.

Chapter Six

Micah
I heard the pipes groan and whine as someone used their bathroom. I wasn't sure if the other guests were in the house and wondered if it were Peyton. I hoped that she would have a chance to relax and take the time to heal. I could see it on her face that she wanted to do everything right. She was feeling her way through life by dipping her toe in front of her. It was like she was a blind woman walking through a mine field.

I wondered if that is what it had been like for her during her marriage. I hated that she even felt like that. I hated that anyone felt that way. I was still musing about it, standing against my kitchen bench when I heard the bell ring above the entrance door. I went out to see Lana come in with her arms filled with bread from her bakery.

I headed for her and unloaded a few of the loaves that were covering her face. "Let me help," I said with a laugh.

Lana laughed in return and handed me off some of the loaves of bread in her arms. I'd started making my own bread for breakfasts when I opened the lodge. But after a while I thought it was better to just buy from Lana. *Why make life harder on me when the bread was better from the bakery?*

"Thank you," I said as I unloaded the bread onto the kitchen bench and took the bags of pastries from Lana's hands.

"That's alright. I saw you have a new guest," she said with a sparkle in her eye. It never ceased to amaze me how this town got their gossip so quickly.

"Yeah, she's been beat to hell," I said. It was no secret in Badger Valley that I opened the rooms up to women who were escaping domestic abuse. For the most part the town welcomed them with open arms and helped to integrate them into the community. It was something that I loved about Badger Valley. It wasn't just a town; it was more like a family.

"Shit," Lana swore with a shake of her head. "Bad?"

I sighed and nodded my head. "The worst we've had for a while," I confirmed.

Lana winced and shook her head. "I hate those assholes that do this to women. They deserve to rot in hell."

"Yeah, they do," I said matching Lana's growl. Most of the town knew about Mom. Sadly, there wasn't a safe place that she could run back then. It wasn't that there weren't people that would have helped her. It was just that most people minded their own business and didn't get involved unless the woman asked.

Everyone knew that Dad beat Mom, but while Mom never complained no one did anything. It wasn't until Dad killed her that something was finally done. But of course, by that time it was too late. I realized that there were many women I wasn't able to save because like my mom they didn't say anything and kept the abuse hidden. But for those that wanted to escape I would do everything I could to help them.

"You're a good guy, Micah," Lana said breaking into my inner thoughts. "If anyone can help her heal, it is you."

I smiled at Lana and nodded my head. I hoped I could help. It was all that I wanted to do. Was to help the women that were able to escape. To give them a safe place to land.

"Well, I best get back to it, those tarts aren't going to cook themselves," Lana said with a grin before she turned and headed for the door.

"Come back and meet Peyton in a few days, she could do with more friends to help her through," I said.

Lana nodded her head and smiled a warm grin. "I will. I'll let her settle in for a few days first."

"Thanks Lana," I replied. Lana waved over her shoulder before she disappeared through the door. The bell tinkling as the front door opened and closed. "We'll keep her safe, Bessy."

The house groaned again as if in agreeance. I smiled and patted the bench as I started to think about the casserole I was going to prepare for that nights meal. I started to pour over the fresh vegetables I'd picked up from the grocery store that morning. Pulling out potatoes, carrots, onions, and turnips. I piled them on the bench, beside the large slab of meat Callum, one of the local hunters had dropped into me.

Soon the broth was bubbling away on the stove, and I was butchering the meat into bite sized pieces. The scent of the casserole floated through the air, and I was humming away to a song that played through my mind. The snow continued to fall silently outside, and the warmth of the fire combined with the kitchen kept the whole house happily warm. Bessy contently moaned now and then as if she was enjoying the delicious scents that filled the air.

Chapter Seven

Peyton

I woke up feeling like I was being embraced in a soft hug. The beautiful aroma of coffee and bacon filtered through my foggy mind. I blinked my eyes open to light pouring through the open curtains. Frowning I glanced at the clock that hung above the dresser and gasped. I'd slept all night. I didn't even have a nightmare. I hadn't slept like that, well in forever.

I sat up slowly. Regretting immediately pulling myself out of the warm embrace the bed seemed to have on me. But my bladder was screaming louder, and my stomach rumbled with hunger. I realized I'd slept through dinner and hadn't eaten since before I left the hospital the day before. I went to the bathroom and took care of business. When I looked in the mirror, I winced at the sight in front of me. The bruises were starting to change from purple to yellow. My eye was still swollen and sore to the touch.

"Alright Bessy, am I allowed out of my room this morning?" I asked with humor threaded through my voice as I tugged on the doorknob. In answer the knob twisted smoothly, and the door opened with a soft creak. I laughed quietly as I shook my head. "You really are living and breathing, aren't you?" The pipes groaned, startling me. Shaking my head, I grabbed the key to my room and locked the door behind me, not that I had anything that would be worth stealing and headed downstairs.

In the dining room the tables were filled with a few other couples, who all glanced up at me as I entered. I considered backing out and heading back to my room. However, my stomach had other ideas as it chose that time to growl again.

"Ah, good morning Peyton," Micah said as he came in through a swinging door that I assumed led to a kitchen, carrying a pot of coffee. "Come and sit down, I've got some bacon and eggs prepared."

I smiled and nodded my head. Sliding into the seat at the table, I did my best not to make eye contact with the other occupants in the room. Low chatter filled my ears, as the other visitors planned what ski slopes they would hit while they were in town.

"Hey, how are you feeling?" Micah asked as he slipped a plate of bacon, toast, and eggs in front of me.

"I've never slept so well," I replied, glancing briefly up at him.

"That's great. Bessy made sure to keep you safe," Micah replied with a chuckle causing me to laugh. I nodded my head. *She sure did.*

"I never rang my parents, I was so tired, that I just fell asleep," I told Micah with a frown. I'd promised Mom and Dad that I would ring them once I arrived at the lodge. But I'd completely forgotten.

"Your dad rang last night. I explained to him that you were asleep and said I'd get you to call him this morning when you woke up," Micah replied.

I sighed and slipped a piece of bacon between my lips. The salty meat filled my taste buds with sheer joy. It didn't take long, and I was engulfing my food. Jason had controlled everything, including what I could eat. It had been so long since I had bacon. I was in ecstasy.

Micah continued to roam through the room filling cups of coffee and chatting to his guests. An elderly couple sat at the table beside me. The woman tried to catch my eye, but I purposely kept my head down. I wasn't ready to answer why I was there or tell my story.

Once the breakfast was finished and Micah was gathering empty plates, the elderly couple stood readying themselves to leave. The woman stopped at my table and gently reached out touching my arm.

"Don't go back to him, never go back to him," she said softly.

I looked up at her and felt my eyes prickle with tears. "I won't," I promised. It was a promise that I knew I could keep. I would never put myself in that position ever again.

The woman smiled and nodded her head. "Good girl." She turned and left with her husband by her side. I watched them leave through the front door.

"They are a lovely couple. Their daughter came here to stay for a while a few years back. They've been visiting every Christmas ever since," Micah explained as he slid into the seat opposite me.

"What happened to their daughter?" I asked.

Micah winced. "She went back to her husband. He beat her to death within weeks of her return."

I groaned. I couldn't help but wonder how often that was the common story. *How many women went back because their partners had such control of them?* I wondered if Jason would try to get me back. I hoped not. I liked to think that I was going to be strong enough not to return. But I just couldn't say.

Chapter Eight

Micah

I was glad when Camilla and George were here to see Peyton. I wasn't close enough to hear what Camilla said to her but knew that she would be pleading for Peyton to stay safe. After the breakfast dishes were in the kitchen, I brought the phone into the dining room so that Peyton could call her dad.

I could hear Peyton on the phone reassuring her dad that she was safe and comfortable. I was glad that she'd slept as well as she did and gave Bessy a gentle pat on the door frame as I walked back into the kitchen to begin on the dishes and to start preparing meat to roast for dinner that night.

The door to the kitchen swung open once I was halfway through putting dishes in the dishwasher. I looked over my shoulder to see Peyton coming in with my phone. "Thank you for letting me use your phone," she said as she placed it down on the bench.

"You're welcome to use it whenever you need," I said returning her smile.

Peyton nodded her head and then looked around the room. One thing I'd learned from working with abused women, often they struggled to meet a person's eyes. Peyton was no different.

"Do you need some help?" she asked.

"Sure, would you mind rinsing those pans for me?" I asked. Peyton's answering smile lit up her face as she went to the sink and began to rinse the fry pans and platters that I used for breakfast.

We worked in a companionable silence for some time until the dishwasher was completely stacked and turned on. Peyton began to wipe down the surfaces, while I pulled out meat and vegetables to prep for dinner.

"What are you making?" she asked looking over my shoulder.

"I'm going to roast up some venison that one of the local hunters brought me," I replied. "Want to help?"

Peyton smiled and nodded her head. I watched as her shoulders relaxed and for the first time since I met her the day before she seemed to be feeling comfortable. I still made sure to keep my distance from her so that she didn't feel crowded. As Peyton cut up vegetables, she attempted to make them as perfect as possible. I didn't say anything, knowing that anything I said could be misconstrued as criticism. Although I recognized criticism as a good thing, I also knew from experience that women who had been through what Peyton had been didn't see criticism as anything healthy.

I scored the meat and sealed it on the stove. Once it was covered in salt and pepper, I took the potatoes that Peyton had cut into perfect cubes and layered them on the bottom of the large oven dish with onion, carrots, and pumpkin. Placing the venison on top of the vegetables I slid it into the giant oven to slow cook for the afternoon.

Silently Peyton cleaned up the scraps and wiped down the bench. She looked around the room and sighed, wiping her hands on her yoga pants.

"What else do you need help with?" she asked.

"Nothing right now," I said glancing at the clock that sat on the wall. It was almost lunch time. We didn't serve lunch at the lodge and normally I would use the time to do bookwork or clean the rooms of those that had checked out. It just happened that on that day we didn't have anyone checking out and I really didn't feel like doing the books.

"Would you like to come and have lunch with me? I was thinking about going to the diner. They have the world's best steak there," I said with a wide smile.

Peyton watched me for a few beats. At first, I thought she was going to decline my offer, but she surprised me when she nodded her head. "I'll go and put some shoes on," she said as she turned and walked quickly up the stairs.

I watched after her as she left. "What do you reckon Bessy? She going to be alright?" I asked quietly.

Bessy's pipes groaned letting me know that she was going to protect Peyton. After a few minutes Peyton returned to the living room wearing a thick sweater over the top of her yoga pants. Her boots sat snugly on her feet. I knew that she was still not going to be warm enough. Even though the diner was literally down the road.

I went to the coat rack and pulled off one of the spare winter jackets I kept there as well as a beanie, scarf, and gloves. "Here put these on. It will be freezing out there," I said with a smile.

Peyton took the jacket from my hands and slipped it on. The jacket pretty much swallowed her. It reached to almost her knees and the sleeves hung off her hands. She lifted the sleeve and brought it to her nose, sniffing in the scent of the old jacket.

Her cheeks blushed slightly when she caught me watching her and she lowered her eyes to the ground. Quickly she slipped the beanie low on her head and wrapped the scarf around her neck. I smiled and swung the front door open. "Look after yourself Bessy," I said as I stepped over the threshold, guiding Peyton down the front stoop and onto the street.

Snow blinked from where it had settled on the sidewalk. The aroma's of the bakery floated through the air, and people milled around doing the last of their Christmas shopping. There was only a week before the big day. Thankfully, I had gone out early to purchase all of my shopping. Not that I had many people to buy for, but I always liked to give to some of the locals and to my guests.

Peyton and I wandered in silence along the street. Peyton's head swiveled taking in everything to be seen. A few times she would slow down in front of a shop window when something caught her eye before moving on. When we arrived at the diner, I swung the door open and guided her in.

The scent of cooking food hit my nostrils the minute I stepped into the diner. "Hey Micah, grab a seat and I'll be with you in a minute," Delilah called. She was an older lady who had worked there for as long as I could remember.

I guided Peyton over to a table in the corner of the room that looked out onto the street. Peyton sat carefully and picked up the menu as she began to peruse it.

"What are you thinking?" I asked.

Peyton pursed her lips and scratched at her chin. I remained silent. I didn't imagine she was allowed to make her own decisions, so this was something that I wanted her to do for herself.

"I don't know what is good," she said. "I'm feeling a bit overwhelmed."

I smiled and nodded my head. "The fried chicken is really good, so is the steak. I guess it depends on how hungry you are."

Peyton looked back down at the menu and sighed. "It's so stupid that I can't even decide what to eat."

"It's not stupid at all honey," Delilah said startling Peyton. "Lots of girls in your position struggle to make decisions when they first leave."

"How did you know?" Peyton asked looking at me to see if I had told anyone.

Delilah chuckled. "Believe me girls look all the same when they have finally left those assholes. Timid, beat to hell and overwhelmed. But they don't realize how strong they really are."

"I don't feel strong," Peyton murmured.

Delilah reached out her hand and stroked the back of Peyton's hair. "You will in time. Do you know how to eat an elephant?" Peyton frowned with confusion and shook her head. "One bite at a time. That is how you will make it through. One minute at a time."

Peyton sighed and relaxed into her seat. I smiled up at Delilah in thanks. Delilah caught my eye and gave me a little wink.

"I think I'll have the chicken sandwich with a side of fries, please," Peyton said.

"Great choice honey, would you like something to drink?" Delilah asked.

"A soda would be great, thank you," Peyton replied, seemingly finding it easier to make the request.

"The usual steak for you Micah?" Delilah asked with a grin. I nodded my head and watched as Delilah ambled off to the kitchen to put our order in.

Peyton breathed out a long breath. "She is nice."

I nodded my head. "She is. Delilah has been around forever and has always reached out to the women that escape to Badger Valley."

"Do you think she has been in my situation?" Peyton questioned glancing over at the older woman as she refilled coffee cups for the locals that sat against the bench.

"That's possible."

Chapter Nine

P eyton

It occurred to me halfway through my lunch, how relaxed I felt with Micah. I couldn't remember a time I ever felt that way about Jason. Even when we were dating as teenagers, he had me on edge. But here I was not worrying about whether I got everything right. I didn't have to be concerned if I dripped some mayonnaise on my shirt. Micah wouldn't care. I didn't know how I knew it, but I knew he wouldn't.

"Tell me about you?" I asked him as I took my final bite of the chicken sandwich and washed it down with a mouthful of soda. The food had been delicious, and I'd practically inhaled the sandwich without breathing.

"Not much to tell really. I grew up in Badger Valley with my parents until I was twelve and then I went into the foster care system. I moved to Anchorage and lived with a few families until I was eighteen and came back here," he said with a shrug.

I knew that there was more to the story that he was holding back. But it wasn't my place to push. Micah would tell me if he wanted me to know. Delilah ambled her way over to the table and started to clear our empty plates.

"What did you think honey? Best chicken sandwich you've ever had?" she asked with a broad smile.

I nodded enthusiastically. It was no lie. The chicken had been moist and delicious. "I think I'm going to be back regularly," I said with a grin.

Delilah tipped her head back and let out a big belly laugh that was contagious. I found myself smiling along with her.

"Make sure you do. You look like you could get some more meat on those bones of yours," she said in a tone that had Mom all over it.

I smiled and nodded my head as Micah slid out of the booth and went to the counter where Delilah rang up our bills. I stood beside the table and watched as Micah and Delilah easily bantered between each other. Micah greeted a few of the people that sat at the counter with a smile and a handshake.

It seemed like I had walked into an alternate reality. I didn't think there would ever be a place where everyone was so warm, friendly, and welcoming, but as I watched the way everyone interacted with Micah, I knew that he was definitely well liked and by association I was getting the same welcome.

The feeling was overwhelming, but strangely comforting at the same time. For the first time since before I met Jason, I felt like I could make a home. That I found my tribe. I had only been in Badger Valley for a day, but it felt like I had been there for much longer.

The bell above the door of the diner jingled and when I glanced over, I saw Maurice the moose rubbing his antlers against the door. Delilah rolled her eyes and chuckled. She reached down under the counter and pulled out a jelly filled donut and headed towards the door.

"Here you go Maurice, you know you're going to get fat if you keep eating these," Delilah said as she handed the huge moose his pastry treat. He snuffled it up and snorted against Delilah's hand. Shaking his head, he turned and left down the street.

"You watch he will be next door looking for more pastries," Micah said with a laugh. I went to the window and watched as Maurice knocked his antlers on the window next to the diner. A man came out and handed him what looked like a croissant. Once again Maurice snuffled it up in one bite and was on his way.

I turned back to Micah and shook my head. "I have never seen anything like it," I said with astonishment.

Micah laughed. "The town has adopted him, or maybe Maurice adopted the town. But either way he is well loved and well fed here."

"I wouldn't leave either if I got pastries everywhere I went too," I said with a giggle.

"I can arrange that," Micah replied flirtatiously with a wink.

My eyes widened and my lips popped open in shock. No man would have dared to flirt with me when I was with Jason. He made sure that everyone knew that I was his property. But Jason wasn't around here. I wasn't his property. And it kind of felt nice to have someone pay attention to me.

I smiled shyly at Micah who smiled down at me and gently put his hand on my lower back. "How about we go and find you some warm clothes that actually fit you?"

I glanced down at the jacket that Micah had lent me. It was huge on me and hung down to my knees. No doubt I looked ridiculous in it, but I liked it. The jacket carried Micah's sent of sugar and cinnamon.

"Would you mind if I just used this one for the winter?" I asked bringing the sleeve up to my nose and sniffing it.

I looked up at Micah through my eyelashes and watched his pupils dilate before he shook his head and licked his bottom lip. When he spoke, his voice was deeper and more husky. "Sure, that would be fine."

Gently taking my hand that wasn't in a cast he led me out of the diner and back towards the lodge. I didn't know what was happening between us, but sometime between last night and finishing lunch at the diner I made the decision that I was going to let my life play out, and if that meant things happening with Micah, I was going to let it happen. I had wasted too much time with Jason. I didn't want to lose any more time on misery.

Chapter Ten

Peyton

The days went on in the same way. I would wake up after a night of dreamless sleep, feeling like I was being held in a warm embrace. I'd join Micah in the kitchen to help him make breakfast and then to prepare dinner. Sometimes Micah would do bookwork while I cleaned the rooms of those that had left that morning.

I couldn't stop smiling. I'd never felt so relaxed before. I spoke to Mom and Dad every day to keep them in the loop. I couldn't wait for Christmas morning, when I knew that they would arrive to join me in Badger Valley. It was the first Christmas I would have had with them since I was a child.

Mom and Dad said that they hadn't heard anything about the case against Jason, only that he was in jail, because he hadn't been able to afford the bail. I was relaxed. I knew that I couldn't stay like this forever, I was going to have to find a job and a home to live in more permanently.

I'd been at the lodge for a week when I found Micah in his office after I finished cleaning one of the rooms and bathroom. He was frowning at the screen of his laptop. Glasses perched on his nose. His blonde hair was tied into a messy bun at the back of his head.

He was a really good-looking guy. So different to Jason. Where Jason's body had been forced to be muscular by hours spent at the gym and pumping his body full of steroids, Micah had a naturally muscular build that was a little soft around the middle. I liked it a lot. The more time I spent with him, the more I would find myself taking notice of all the little things. Like how his nose would scrunch when he was concentrating. Or how he would lick his bottom lip as he kneaded pastry.

I found it all sexy. I didn't think I was ever going to even want to get close to another man after Jason. But with every moment I spent with Micah, I found myself thinking less about Jason and wanting to get to know Micah more.

Micah glanced up at me and leaned back in his chair with a groan. He twisted cracking his neck and stretching his arms above his head. "I hate paperwork," he groaned.

I giggled and entered his office. Reaching out with my one unplastered arm I began to knead his neck and shoulder. Micah dropped his head forward with a moan. "Oh, I'll keep you if you do that," he said with a chuckle.

I laughed and continued to knead at the tight muscles. "I'm not much good with only one hand."

"It still feels good," he said huskily.

My tongue ran over my bottom lip as the atmosphere seemed to thicken around us. I honestly didn't know what I was doing or if this was even a good idea. But I couldn't seem to stop my heart. It wanted what it wanted, and I felt powerless to stop it.

Micah placed his hand over mine stopping the massage and turning in his seat to look at me. "How are you doing? *Really*?" he asked.

I looked down into his dark blue eyes. "I'm honestly doing well. I'm surprised. You have made me feel so free here."

Micah smiled and nodded his head. "I'm glad. I want you to heal. I want you to enjoy your freedom. I want you to see that here you are safe."

Micah stroked his thumb over my hand that he still held in his. Butterflies were taking flight in my stomach. "I. um, I don't know what I'm doing Micah and I'm probably going to mess everything up, but I really like you."

Micah didn't say anything but continued to watch me. He studied my face. His hand warm engulfing mine. "I like you too. But" he started, and I felt my heart start to plummet into my stomach. "I'm worried that this is moving too fast for you."

I sucked in a deep breath and slowly let it out. "Micah I never loved Jason. I fell out of love with him the first time he hit me. We were together since we were fifteen. He first hit me when I was sixteen. But I felt like I was stuck. By the time he did this to me, I hated him. I prayed he would one day just kill me so it could be over."

Micah winced at my words. He slowly stood from his seat and let go of my hand. Gently he ran his fingers up over my cheeks and held my face carefully. The bruises were barely visible now. He looked down into my eyes.

"So, if I was to kiss you, it would be alright?" he said licking his bottom lip nervously. I followed the movement before looking up into his eyes.

"Yes," I replied huskily.

Slowly, giving me enough time to back out, Micah leaned down and pressed his lips against mine. His lips were warm and soft. The prickle of stubble on his chin scratched at my skin deliciously. I opened my lips and licked across the seam of his mouth. My eyes closed and I sunk into the kiss. Micah tangled his tongue with mine. He didn't move his hands from my cheeks as he continued to kiss me more passionately than I had ever been kissed before. When he pulled back, I was out of breath. I looked up at Micah with a shy smile.

"I think we need to do that again," I whispered. Micah barked out a laughed and pulled me into his chest.

"Yeah, we do," he agreed as he pressed a kiss to the top of my head.

For the first time since I could remember I felt completely happy. Completely whole. It was a unique feeling. One that I loved and didn't want to give up any time soon.

Chapter Eleven

Micah

My brain was screaming at me that I was pushing Peyton into something that I shouldn't, but I couldn't seem to stop myself. The minute I felt her soft warm lips against mine and her tongue slide into my mouth I was done. She was beautiful, no one could deny that. The longer I spent with her the more I had seen her open up and when she laughed her whole demeanor changed.

Peyton was starting to come out of her shell and morphing into the most beautiful woman I had ever laid eyes on. Not just physically, but it was like there was a light inside her that oozed out of her pores and engulfed everything around her. No one was able to ignore her. I watched others when we walked down the streets of Badger Valley, in the way they turned their heads just to keep staring at her for that bit longer. Everyone wanted to know Peyton and have her turn her attention on them.

She was like a magnet pulling me towards her. The last thing I wanted to do though was rush her into something she might not be ready for. It had only been a week ago that she was in the hospital, having had the hell beat out of her by her husband. I knew that she was telling the truth when she said she didn't love him. I couldn't imagine any woman would really love any man that hit them. But I was still nervous.

This could all go wrong, and it would be my fault. I was just going to have to make sure we went slowly. I didn't want her to feel like she was getting trapped by me. I wanted Peyton to be able to have her freedom.

When Peyton pulled back from me, she looked up at me, her pupils were blown, and her lips were puffy from my kisses. Her chin was red from the way my stubble had brushed on her skin.

"Wow," she giggled. I chuckled as I watched her, all of the emotions that ran over her face were so apparent. But the one I didn't see was panic or concern.

"How about we get a start on preparing some dinner," I suggested, really not wanting to leave the room or her body.

Peyton smiled and nodded her head. The tip of her tongue poked out and ran over her bottom lip. It took everything I had not to pull her back into me and kiss her again. There was going to be plenty of time for kisses and more. I cleared my throat and pulled back.

"Right, dinner," I said clearing my voice again. Peyton laughed but allowed me to take her hand and lead her out of the office and into the kitchen.

We were busy cutting up vegetables and meat for a stew. We were only a few days out from Christmas, and I was expecting a full house. I had already ordered pies from Lana for our Christmas meal. I had two large turkeys in the freezer ready to pull out and I would top up our vegetables. We were set to go. Like every Christmas since they lost their daughter, Camilla and George were staying here. Christmas and Lucy's birthday was hard for them. I knew that they headed to the beach for her birthday, but every Christmas they came here.

"I will have to cut the Christmas tree this afternoon and then we can decorate it," I said conversationally as we chopped vegetables.

Peyton looked over at me and grinned. "That sounds fun, I haven't had a Christmas tree since I was a kid."

"Then this will be great. I'll get the decorations out of the attic after we have finished prepping the stew and then I'll go out and cut down a tree to bring back," I said feeling my excitement mounting.

Every year since I bought the lodge, I set up a Christmas tree. It only ever held lights and baubles. On the baubles was written the woman's name that had come here, whether they went on to freedom or like Lucy passed away. It had started with my mother's name. When the first girl,

Carly, came to stay, I decided to add each woman's name as an honor to them.

Some of the women occasionally still came and stayed over Christmas. This year however, it would just be Peyton. Our tree though would be filled. Every year I always stood amazed at the amount of names that decorated the tree. Some of those like Lucy, broke my heart. I hated knowing that she went back and was killed by her husband. But others like Carly and Taryn went on to live amazing lives. Taryn realized that she preferred women. She married her wife a few years ago and together they now had three daughters of their own.

Every year I made it a point to send each of the women a Christmas card and I usually got quite a few in return, updating me on their lives. I loved hearing about the success stories. Of course, not every woman was able to have a life as wonderful as Taryn. Some went on to go from abusive man to abusive man. Those cases broke my heart. And they always knew that they had a place available for them at the lodge.

It had only been a couple of times that I had girls come back repeatedly for a few years. Siobhan was one of those women. She was only sixteen when she first came here. Forced to marry a cousin, of all people. She got free, came to the lodge, and stayed for a few months. Then some tourist came in and swept her off her feet. Off she went with him, only to discover that he was just as abusive, and she came back.

Each time she returned I watched the light in her eyes die that little bit more. The last visit was two years ago. She left the lodge along with whatever cash I had in the cashbox and a few items she could no doubt sell. Siobhan had fallen into a crowd that was ruled by drugs. I tried to encourage her to go to rehab, but she was determined she was fine. Since that day, I'd never heard from her again. It didn't stop me thinking about her. Hoping that she was safe and that one day she would get the help she needed.

Never before had I ever been interested in more with one of the women that came to stay here. In fact, I had made it a rule to never get romantically involved with any of the women. Yet there was something about Peyton that I hadn't been able to resist. My heart wanted her. I couldn't explain it. But I craved this girl that made my life so complete.

Chapter Twelve

Peyton

I couldn't remember the last time I'd been this excited for Christmas. After we finished getting dinner prepped, Micah went up into the attic and pulled down the decorations for the tree. Dressed in the jacket I had borrowed from Micah, thermals, thick pants and boots I tromped through the snow by Micah's side as we went in search of a suitable tree to use as a Christmas tree.

My life was so different compared to last year. Last year I was married to a man who beat the hell out of me. We didn't have a Christmas tree, there were no decorations, no Christmas turkey. I wasn't allowed to even ring my mom and dad to wish them a happy holidays. Instead, I sat on the couch beside Jason while he drank and watched football reruns.

But this year was different. This year not only was in constant contact with my parents and had all the decorations and beautiful food I could ask for. I was slowly getting to know a new man. A man that I seemed to be able to trust implicitly. One that showed me more affection and care than Jason ever did in our whole relationship.

I couldn't wait to see where this was going to lead. It didn't mean I wasn't nervous. I was scared that it could all go wrong. But for the first time in an exceedingly long time, I was genuinely happy. I felt relaxed. I wasn't striving for perfection because Micah didn't expect that from me. He took me as I came.

"What do you think of this one?" Micah said as he stopped in front of a fairly large pine. I looked up at the spindles that were covered in snow.

Smiling I nodded my head. "It's perfect."

Micah grinned and leaned forward pressing a chaste kiss to my lips. I licked my bottom lip and watched as he turned back to work, bringing the chainsaw to life, and cutting into the trunk of the pine.

"Stand back, it's going to come down any second," Micah shouted. I stepped back so that I was behind Micah when the final crack sounded, and the tree tumbled to the ground with a soft thud. Snow floated around it and quickly settled back on the ground.

After turning off the chainsaw, Micah picked up the trunk of the pine and started to walk back towards the lodge. I followed behind with a skip in my step. As we rounded the corner of the lodge Maurice the moose was standing watching us.

I giggled expecting him to come and demand baked goods from Micah, but instead he just stood and watched us as we entered the lodge. Micah dragged the tree into the shared living room, beside the huge wood fire. I stripped out of my jacket, as the warmth of the fire caused my cheeks to sting. I reached out my hands towards the fire and allowed the warmth to spread over my entire body.

Micah had already prepared a large bucket and tree holder in the corner, so it didn't take long, and the tree was standing and in place ready to be decorated.

"What do you think?" Micah asked once he had the tree in place.

"I think it looks amazing. I can't wait to see it all decorated," I said with a grin.

Micah smiled down at me and started stripping out of his jacket. "Let me get this off and then we can start. Do you want to start pulling out the lights?"

I nodded my head dragging my eyes off Micah as he stripped out of his jacket. I opened the box that was marked as Christmas lights. Pulling out the carefully wrapped string of lights I easily untangled them. By the time I had them all out, Micah was standing beside me.

"Give me one end and you take the other," Micah instructed. "You do the lower branches and I'll do the top."

I nodded and started to wrap the lights around the lower branches of the tree. Together we worked in silence stringing lights and the baubles with each name of the women who had come to stay in the lodge.

With the last bauble hung, Micah stood back and looked at the tree. He reached out a hand and pulled me gently into his side. "There is just two more things that are needed."

I glanced up at him with confusion. I couldn't see anything that was needed. Micah reached into the box and pulled out another bauble. This was one coloured in iridescent purples and pinks. It almost looked like a sunset over an ocean. He brought the glass bauble towards me.

"You need to write your name on here," Micah said with a smile.

I chewed on my bottom lip and nodded my head, taking the gold marker from his hand and the bauble. Carefully as I could I wrote my name in a pretty script across the bauble. Micah took it back and blew on the marker. His eyes never left mine.

Without a word, Micah turned back to the tree at placed the bauble at the very top. I blinked back tears at the sentimentality of it all.

"What is the other thing that needs to be hung?" I asked.

Micah chuckled and reached into the box again pulling out decorative mistletoe. "This," he said.

I laughed and followed him to the entrance of the living room and foyer. Micah hung the mistletoe on the door frame and pulled me into his arms. "It's only right that I kiss a pretty girl under the mistletoe."

I giggled and stood on my toes as I pressed my lips against Micah's in a firm kiss. My eye lids drooped, and I wound my unplastered arm around Micah's neck. His hands held my hips firmly and he tilted his head as he deepened the kiss, groaning as our tongues danced together erotically.

Micah's hands skimmed down over my ass. I could feel his length press against my stomach. I had never wanted anyone more than I wanted Micah at that moment. I pressed my body against him tighter. Micah broke the kiss, breathlessly he pressed his forehead against mine.

"If I don't stop now, I don't think I will be able to," he whispered.

"I don't want you to," I replied.

Micah's eyes widened and he lowered his teeth into his bottom lip. "Are you sure?"

I nodded my head and licked at his top lip. Slowly I ran my hand down over his chest to the bulge in his jeans. Micah groaned and thrust into my hand. Wordlessly he took me by the hand and turned, leading me towards his bedroom that sat nestled on the ground floor at the back of the lodge. My mind whirled, I was going to do this. I was going to allow a man to show me what love was meant to feel like.

Chapter Thirteen

Micah

I was nervous. I was no virgin, I never found it hard to find a willing bed partner when I wanted it. But this was different. I wanted to show Peyton that this wasn't just a quick fuck. I wanted more than that. Her hand was warm in mine as I led her into my bedroom. The king-sized bed taking up most of the small room that I had chosen as my own.

I turned to face Peyton who was watching me with big eyes. Her pupils were blown, and I could see from the look on her face that she had no intention of ending this. She wanted me as much as I wanted her.

"If at any stage you want to stop, then you just say so, and it ends," I said looking down into her face.

Peyton's teeth sunk into her bottom lip, and she nodded her head. "I want you, Micah."

I groaned. Her voice had become husky with need. My cock twitched in my jeans at the look on her face. This woman was everything. I bent and pressed my lips against hers in a firm kiss. Peyton's body melted against mine. Her uninjured hand stroked over the plains of my back and chest.

With trembling hands, I reached for the hem of her shirt, lifting it, only breaking the kiss long enough that we could get her shirt off over her head. Peyton wasn't wearing a bra beneath. Something I had noticed more than once. Her pinkened nipples pebbled in the cool air. I kissed slowly down over Peyton's cheeks and throat. Peyton moaned. Slowly I moved towards her chest. Circling her nipple with my tongue while gently plucking the other between my thumb and finger.

Peyton gasped and rocked forward, pressing her breasts harder against my face. Her uninjured hand stroked through my hair, holding me tight against her. "That feels so good," she whispered.

I moaned against her chest as I kissed my way over to the other nipple, rolling it with my tongue. It hardened further in my mouth. Kissing back up to Peyton's throat, I looked into her eyes that were watching me lazily with pleasure all over her face. Taking her hand, I guided her over to the bed.

Once she was standing beside the bed, I reached down and slipped my shirt over my head. Peyton's teeth sunk into her bottom lip as she watched me. I popped the button on my jeans and released the zipper. Pushing my jeans down over my thighs and to my feet, I kicked them off, so I was standing in my boxers in front of her. My cock tented my boxers and Peyton's eyes were drawn to it, causing it to twitch in my pants.

"Can I touch you?" she whispered.

I groaned as I nodded my head. Tentatively Peyton reached out and stroked my length through my boxers eliciting a long moan from my lips. "You're so big," she whispered almost to herself.

I chuckled. "You just have little hands," I answered making her giggle.

I reached out and slowly began to slide her yoga pants down over her thighs and to her ankles. I lowered to my knees and slipped her feet out of the pants. Leaning forward I pressed light kisses against the inside of her knees.

"Sit on the bed," I directed.

When Peyton sat down, the wet patch that had formed on the crotch of her panties was apparent. I groaned as I spread her legs open and pressed featherlight kisses against the inside of her ankle, up along her calves until I reached her knees. I skimmed my hands up the outside of her thighs. Peyton moaned and writhed lightly on the bed beneath me. Smiling up at her I continued my torturous slow kisses along the inside of her thighs.

Peyton's breathing was coming in pants by the time I reached her apex. I pressed my nose against her centre and breathed in her arousal. Groaning, I skimmed my nose on the outside of her panties, over her folds to the bundle of nerves.

Peyton gasped and ground her hips harder against my face. Chuckling I lifted my head and took the edge of her panties, sliding them down over her hips and thighs. I leaned back on my knees so that I could slip them off her feet. I tossed her panties aside, before skimming my hands up over her thighs again and spreading her open for me.

Her dark curls were glistening with her arousal. Groaning I couldn't wait any longer. I draped her legs over my shoulders and kissed against her pussy. Sliding my tongue through her crease. Peyton's fingers threaded through my hair and her hips ground her pussy against me. Her honey coated my tongue, and I knew I was done, I wasn't going to be able to get enough.

I licked at her bud, feeling her pussy tighten against my fingers as I slowly slid them in and out of her. Peyton's moans filled the air, and the scent of her arousal filled my senses. Crooking my fingers, Peyton let out a long shrill cry and her entire body tightened around me. Her thighs clamped the sides of my head. Her fingers tightened in my hair, and she cried out my name over and over as her juices coated my tongue and chin.

I continued to slide my fingers in and out of her prolonging her orgasm for as long as possible. Once her thighs loosened and she released my hair, I glanced up. Peyton's cheeks were pink, and her eyes darkened. She looked down at me through hooded lids.

"I need you inside me," she groaned.

It was all I needed. I tore my boxers from my body and moved up the bed above her. Peyton locked her ankles over my lower back and with her uninjured hand she held onto my arm. "I'm probably not going to last long," I admitted.

Peyton smiled and nodded her head. I glanced down at her centre as I slid the head of my cock through her wet folds. Peyton moaned and her pussy contracted beneath me. Slowly I pushed into her entrance, feeling the walls of her pussy pull me in all the way. Peyton and I moaned simultaneously once I was completely seated inside her.

Slowly I started to roll my hips, grinding against her. I couldn't take my eyes off her. She was beautiful. Peyton's head was thrown back. Her eyes rolled and her thighs shook beneath me. Every moan that escaped her rosy lips brought me closer to the edge. It took everything in me to hold off long enough to ensure that Peyton reached that precipice once again.

Her pussy began to grip me tight, and I could feel her starting to milk me. I pressed my thumb against her clit as I started to move harder inside her. Peyton's eyes shot open, and she cried out. Her legs locked tighter around my hips as I thrust in and out of her. Pleasure was building in the base of my spine, and I knew I wasn't going to be able to hold back much longer. My balls tightened.

"Oh God, Micah," Peyton screamed before her eyes rolled in her head, and it was all I needed. My balls tightened and pleasure took over as I filled her with splashes of cum after cum.

The only sound as we came back to reality was our heavy breaths. Carefully I rolled off Peyton and laid on her side. Peyton rolled onto her side and pressed her face against my chest.

"Wow," she whispered.

"You can say that again," I said with a chuckle.

Peyton giggled and she gently stroked up and down over my chest. Our moment though was interrupted by a pervert moose knocking on my window telling us that we had been watched the entire time. Peyton fell back on the bed into fits of giggles when she realized what had happened.

"Maurice, you are a pervert," I said with a shake of my head. Maurice almost seemed to smile as he turned from the window and wandered further into the yard.

Chapter Fourteen

Peyton

My whole body felt completely satisfied. I was aching slightly between my legs, but it was a delicious ache. One I'd never known before. One I wanted to experience again and again. Micah and I had got busy with Christmas preparations during the day, but every night we spent hours rolling in the sheets, making love in various positions. I didn't realize sex could be as amazing as what I had experienced in just a couple of days with Micah.

Christmas morning, I woke up feeling excited. We were expecting a few people to join us for lunch. Including Mom and Dad who had flown in especially to see us. I couldn't wait to see them. I rolled out of bed, quickly showering, and taking care of my bathroom needs before bouncing into the kitchen that was already filled with scents of bacon, eggs, and freshly baked bread.

Micah was busy working, while bacon sizzled on the stove. I kissed him between his shoulders as I entered the kitchen. Micah glanced over his shoulder and smiled warmly at me.

"Merry Christmas gorgeous girl," he said with a wide smile.

"Best Christmas ever," I grinned in returned.

Micah chuckled and pressed a quick kiss against my lips. "What is this?" I heard Mom's voice say with a smile from the kitchen door.

I giggled and went to take Mom into my arms. "I'm so glad you're here."

"I'm glad I'm here too," Mom said stepping back and looking down at me. "You look so happy. Alaska has been good for you I see."

Dad was busy glaring at Micah. I knew that they would be concerned that I was jumping into another relationship so quickly after Jason. But I also knew that once they got to know Micah, they would see what a good guy he was. He was the complete opposite to Jason.

Dad broke his glare to glance down at me. "I hope you are looking after yourself."

I giggled again and nodded my head. "I am," I said with a roll of my eyes. "Dad he is a good guy. I promise."

Dad looked into my face for a few beats before he nodded his head. He looked back towards Micah who was watching everything. Dad reached out and shook Micah's hand. "If you dare lay a violent hand on my daughter, I won't hesitate to kill you. I won't let her go through that bullshit again."

Micah nodded his head. "I appreciate that sir. I promise I will never lay a hand on Peyton."

Dad continued to stare at Micah before he nodded his head again. I knew that it was going to take time before Dad would be convinced that Micah was a good guy. But I just hoped that he would keep an open mind and Micah's actions would show him the truth.

"Why don't you take your parents to their rooms, and then breakfast should be ready," Micah said with a smile.

I nodded and took Dad's hand, leading them out of the room and up the stairs towards the bedroom that was beside the one I had been using. Once I opened the door, Mom and Dad followed me into the room.

"Promise me you are being safe Peyton," Dad said with a sigh.

I looked over at him and reached out taking his hand in mine. "I promise Dad. Micah is so different to Jason. I had no intention of getting involved with anyone. But it just happened. He is a good guy."

Dad continued to watch me. Tears welled in his eyes, and he cleared his throat. "I hope so," he replied croakily. "I don't ever want to face the possibility of losing you again like I did. It just about killed me."

I felt my own tears start to prickle at my eyes. I walked into Dad's arms and held him tight as a sob bubbled from my throat.

"I'm sorry I didn't walk away sooner. I'm sorry I let it go on for so long," I cried into my dad's neck.

Dad held me by the shoulders and looked down into my eyes, shaking his head firmly. "No," he said with a growl. "Don't ever apologize for that. What Jason did to you, was not your fault at all. I just am always going to worry about you. You are my little girl."

"I love you Dad," I said as I pulled him back into a tight hug.

"I love you too sweetheart," he said into my hair. I felt Mom wrap her arms around both of us as we stood in a firm embrace. One that I hadn't experienced in many years. I was glad to have them back in my life again.

Chapter Fifteen

Micah

Joseph, Peyton's father was intimidating. The way he glared at me I wasn't sure if he was going to punch me or hug me. It'd filled my gut with nerves. His warning was completely expected. I would've reacted the same way.

"Something smells delicious in here," Lana said as she bustled in through the back door with arm loads of bread.

"Breakfast," I answered taking the bread out of her arms. "Did you want some?"

Lana shook her head as she stole a piece of crispy bacon off the plate on the bench and slipped it into her mouth. "No, I've got to get back. I'm just doing a quick lot of deliveries then I'm starting on my own Christmas lunch."

I thanked her and laughed as she stole another piece of bacon before slipping out the back door with a wave over her shoulder. Rolling my eyes, I quickly fried up some extra bacon to replace the stolen pieces. I could hear people starting to file into the dining room.

Peyton was happily greeting people and introducing her parents to our visitors. She had fit in so well here. People seemed to love her. And she had a way with people. She smiled and chatted happily. Certainly, nothing like that scared girl that first came here that couldn't even make eye contact. She had only been here for almost two weeks and her personality had changed so much.

I picked up the plates of bacon and eggs and pushed through the kitchen door. Camilla and George were sitting at the table with Peyton's parents Joseph and Arabella. There were a couple of other visitors sitting at other tables chatting with each other. The atmosphere was warm and festive. Everyone wore a smile on their faces. For the first time in a long time, it was a Christmas that I wasn't just going through the paces, but I was truly going to enjoy it.

"Merry Christmas everyone," I called as I started to place plates down in front of our guests.

A chorus of Merry Christmas was returned to me. Peyton followed me back into the kitchen and grabbed a couple of plates and balanced them on her arms, before turning towards the dining room and sitting them down in front of people with a smile.

Once everyone had a plate of food, I took my seat at Peyton's side. "So, Joseph and Arabella, what do you think of our young Micah here?" George asked with a smile in his voice.

I groaned and wanted to sink under the table. "I would like him a lot better if he wasn't kissing my daughter," Joseph growled, causing George to bark out a laugh.

"Well, if Peyton was to date any man, Micah would be on the top of my list," George replied glancing over at me. "He is like a son to me. From the day that our Lucy came here. We might not have Lucy in our lives anymore, but I couldn't imagine a Christmas without Micah."

Camilla nodded her head and sniffed, dabbing at her eyes. Arabella reached over the table took Camilla's hand, giving it a squeeze. "Your daughter came here like Peyton did to?" Arabella asked.

Camilla nodded again and wiped at her eyes. "Yes. But unlike Peyton, she went back to her ex-husband. Unfortunately, it was the worst decision she could have made."

"Oh god, I'm so sorry," Arabella said as her own eyes welled with tears.

Camilla squeezed Arabella's hand. "It's why we come here every Christmas. It hurts to spend it alone, knowing our daughter isn't around anymore. So, we come here and spend it with Micah. He has always made us feel at home." Camilla looked over at Joseph. "I can guarantee that Peyton is very safe with this young man. And if Peyton turned his head, then I know that she is one incredibly special young lady. Many women have tried over the years, but none have ever succeeded. But the minute I saw you Peyton, I knew that you were the one. Plus, Bessy loves you."

"Bessy?" Camilla asked with a look of confusion on her face.

"The house," Peyton replied with a laugh. "She is a living breathing house." As if in reply to Peyton's statement the pipes groaned, causing the whole table to erupt into laughter.

"Well, son, it seems you come with some high recommendations," Joseph began. "It is going to take a long time for me to trust that any man is going to treat my daughter right, after that asshole. But I'm willing to give you a shot."

Joseph reached out his hand to shake. This time his grip wasn't bone crushing and threatening but one that said welcome to the family. I smiled at him and nodded my head. "Thank you. That means a lot to me. I promise to treat your daughter like the queen she is."

"That's all I can ask," Joseph replied before tucking back into his breakfast.

Before long we were all filling up on breakfast and chatting about Christmas's past. The atmosphere was relaxed, and laughter flowed. This really was going to be a Christmas to remember.

Chapter Sixteen

Peyton

Everything was perfect. Everyone was happy, the food was delicious, and the drinks were flowing. Even Dad and Micah were getting along fabulously. I couldn't imagine a better Christmas. It was exactly what I would've wanted.

I was stacking the last of the dishes into the dishwasher after lunch. Mom and Dad had decided to go for a walk to window shop. While George and Camilla retired for an afternoon nap. The other guests were either milling around in front of the fire, or out sightseeing. Micah was putting the last of the scraps in the trash and getting ready to take it outside.

"Did you have a good day so far?" he asked.

I looked up at Micah and smiled broadly. "It is the best Christmas I've ever experienced," I enthused.

Micah chuckled. "Good," he replied as he pressed a quick kiss to my lips, before taking the trash out and heading for the back door.

Suddenly I heard Micah shouting. I couldn't understand what he was saying, but fear gripped me. I slowly crept towards the back door. I could hear another voice. It was too low to understand what they were saying. But I recognized that voice anywhere. Jason.

Panic hit my stomach and nausea rolled over me. *I thought he was still in jail. No one told me that he was out. How could he be here?* I turned back to the kitchen searching for something. My hands were shaking, my knees felt like they were going to give out on me. If he'd followed me, I knew that there was no way he was going to let me go.

If I didn't get away from him, I was going to die at his hands. I pulled open the drawers and found a butchers knife. Pulling it out with shaking hands I pressed myself against the bench, facing the door. With wide eyes I listened as Micah's shouts became louder.

It didn't take long before I saw Jason dragging Micah in through the back door. Jason's eyes were almost black with anger. He glared around the room. His teeth bared in a snarl. He looked more like a feral animal than a human.

"Hello sweetheart," Jason sneered. I thrust the knife out in front of me. Jason cocked his head to the side and laughed. "What do you intend to do with that sweetheart?"

"Go away Jason," I said as firmly as I could. But even to my ears I sounded weak.

"That's not going to happen sweetheart," he growled. "I'm not leaving without my wife."

"I'm not your wife anymore Jason. I ended our marriage when you landed me in hospital," I said feeling a little bit of strength build inside me.

Jason laughed again and shook his head. "No, see, that's where you are wrong," he continued to sneer. "I tell you when our marriage ends."

Jason lifted his hand from behind Micah's back and showed me that he had a gun in the palm of his hand. He pressed the steel barrel against Micah's temple. Without taking his eyes off me Jason clicked the safety.

"No, Jason, please," I begged, feeling tears well in my eyes. Micah's eyes were wide with panic, and I could see the fear all over his face.

"Have you been fucking him?" Jason spat. His spittle coating the side of Micah's face.

I shook my head rapidly. "No Jason. Only you. I've only ever been with you."

Jason continued to glare at me, watching for the lie to cross my face. Whatever he saw it must have satisfied him. Jason stepped forward towards me, the gun still held tight against Micah's temple.

"Put the knife down, and come with me," Jason demanded in a low and threatening voice that didn't broker argument. I didn't want to obey but I knew if I didn't, he would kill Micah and anyone else that tried to stop him.

I glanced at Micah who gave a small shake of his head. *What choice did I have?* I wasn't going to stand by and let Jason kill the man that I knew I was very quickly falling in love with. That wasn't going to happen. I placed the knife on the bench beside me without taking my eyes off Jason.

I reached out and took Jason's hand. Suddenly a crack filled the room and deafened me as Jason lowered the gun and shot. Micah screamed and fell to the ground. I screamed in horror. I didn't have time to stop and check on Micah as Jason dragged me from the back door to the front of the lodge.

We were halfway to the road when Mom and Dad turned from the sidewalk onto the driveway. Mom was smiling and laughing at something Dad said to her. Dad was the first to see the problem. Mom noticed Dad's reaction and gasped.

"What the fuck are you doing?" Dad growled at Jason.

Jason ignored Dad and pointed his gun towards Mom. "Please Jason don't shoot them, I'm coming with you."

"Peyton no, you can't," Mom cried.

"I have to Mom, please," I replied, trying to convey to her the situation that I was in. I couldn't let Jason kill anyone that I loved. It was bad enough that he'd shot Micah. I just hoped that the shot was enough to rouse the guests and they would get Micah the help he needed. I sent out a tiny prayer that Micah would be alright.

"Yeah Mom, she has to," Jason sneered as he tightened his fist on my arm in a bruising hold.

Jason lowered the gun and continued to drag me towards the road without looking back. I looked around but couldn't see his car anywhere. The streets were empty of all cars. Everyone at home or away with family to celebrate the holidays. All I could hope for was that Mom and Dad would be able to get help before Jason got too far away.

"Come on," Jason growled as he continued to drag me down the sidewalk. I had to jog to keep up with him. I continued to stare around the street in hope that the police would find me. That might be anyone that might be able to save me.

We rounded the corner and I saw that his car was nestled among some pines. From what I could see he'd been parked there for some time. Snow settled on the surface of the car. Jason didn't slow down as he continued to drag me towards the car.

I tripped over twigs and uneven ground. Jason's hold prevented me from falling. His jaw was held tight, and I knew that I was going to have an imprint of his fingers on my bicep. Suddenly what sounded like a roar deafened me. I turned just in time to see Maurice with his antlers lowered charging towards us.

Jason turned, he pointed the gun, but he was too slow. Maurice's antler caught Jason in the chest and lifted him into the air. I watched in horror as Jason was flung across the roof of his car and landed with a gut churning thud against the trunk of a large pine. Maurice didn't stop. He lowered his head again and charged Jason. Over and over, I watched in horror as Maurice continued to pummel Jason's lifeless body, until every bone had to be crushed.

"Peyton," I heard in the distance. I didn't turn my head as I stared at Jason's unrecognizable, bloody, and broken body. "Peyton."

I turned just as Dad pulled me into his arms. "Are you hurt?" he asked. Panic laced his voice, and his eyes were wild with fear.

I looked at Dad and shook my head. Tears streamed down over my cheeks. Fear caused my entire body to tremble. "Micah?" I whispered.

"He is going to be fine. Just a flesh wound in the leg, the doctor is with him now, patching him up. But it is you that I'm worried about. Did Jason hurt you?" Dad continued.

"No, no he didn't hurt me. Is he dead?" I asked.

Dad looked over my shoulder at the crumpled body of my ex-husband. "Yes, he's dead. A giant moose saved you."

"Maurice," I replied. Dad looked down at me with a small shake of his head, confusion was etched into his face. I knew I probably sounded like I was going mad. "The moose. His name is Maurice. He likes pastries."

Dad chuckled and nodded. "Right well, I'll have to buy him a whole pile of them," he replied as he slowly started to walk me down to the sidewalk where I could see police starting to arrive.

After I spoke to Brody and explained to him what happened, Dad led me back to the lodge. Doctor Ashburn was wrapping Micah's leg. It felt like everything was moving in slow motion. My ears felt like I was hearing underwater. The blood that pumped through my body whooshed inside my head. My body trembled, in a combination of fear and adrenalin. Jason again had come so close to killing me. But like Micah promised, the town kept me safe.

"Peyton, oh god Peyton, you are alright?" Micah called when he saw me.

A sob fell from my lips, and I ran from Dad's arms and into Micah's open arms. "He shot you," I cried.

"I'm fine, it just nicked me," he answered. "But you, are you okay?"

I nodded my head and looked into Micah's eyes. "He's dead. Maurice, he killed him."

Micah held my cheeks and stroked my face. "Good."

I nodded again and looked over at Micah's leg. The bandage was bulky, but the Doctor assured me that Micah would be fine. He just needed a couple of days of rest. After Doctor Ashburn checked me over, he left. Brody came and took our statements. Soon enough we were left alone. I couldn't believe that it was over. Not for just a while. But forever. Jason was dead. I thought maybe I should feel some kind of sadness. But inside I felt nothing but relief.

The next day, Dad came in with his arms full of pastries. "What is that for?" Micah asked sounding amused. He was sat out on the couch with his leg up.

"Maurice. He saved my daughter," Dad said proudly. "And some for you too son. You took a bullet for my daughter. If that doesn't prove to me your worthiness, I don't know what will."

I smiled up at Dad. It was going to take me some time before the shock and fear that Jason had built up in me with his last and final visit, but I knew that with Micah by my side I would make it through. I linked my fingers with Micah and glanced over at him. Micah lifted our joined hands and kissed my knuckles.

"How about a kiss for the invalid?" he asked.

I giggled and leaned over him carefully, pressing a kiss against his lips. Yeah, I was going to be simply fine.

The end...

Don't miss out!

Visit the website below and you can sign up to receive emails whenever S L Davies publishes a new book. There's no charge and no obligation.

https://books2read.com/r/B-A-NZRR-HFIDC

BOOKS 2 READ

Connecting independent readers to independent writers.

Did you love *Christmas Escape*? Then you should read *Second Chances*[1] by S L Davies!

[2]

A horrific domestic violent attack leaves Tara's family dead and her left to pick up the pieces, surrounded by nothing but darkness.Tara didn't think she would ever love again, let alone trust another man after Tommy nearly destroyed her. However, with the help from Brock, her childhood friend and one of Tommy's victims, she sees that sometimes life is full of second chances.**This is a dark book, with heavy triggers, including domestic violence, rape and abuse. Suited to 18+**

Read more at https://www.amazon.com/~/e/B0832T8F7Z.

---

1. https://books2read.com/u/4D6WMQ

2. https://books2read.com/u/4D6WMQ

Also by S L Davies

Breeding Facility
Memphis
Bacchus
Coltrane
Pax
Raiden
Nash
Breeding Facility

Devil's Advocates
Lynx
Israel
Jai
Jasper
Arley
Zion
Oakland

KINK
Gunner

Newlyn
Aina
Freya
Tanquil

Obsidian Mechanics
Donte
Atticus
Boden

Onyx Rebels
Onyx Rebels Prologue
Hawke
Rison
Bandit
Butler
Nova

Rigby Brothers
Asher
Burgess
Macklin
Drake
Jericho
Obsidian

Schiavu
Schiavu

Shifter Ink
Brenton
Chase
Orion
Sloane

Stolen
Stolen
The Murphy Princess
Little Warrior

Wild Claw Pack
Connell

Standalone
Sisters Revenge
Killer Love
Soldiers At War
Second Chances
Bunny
Caged

By The Sword
The Cult
Rising Sun
Forbidden Bound
Christmas Escape
Executioner

Watch for more at https://www.amazon.com/~/e/B0832T8F7Z.

About the Author

S L Davies is an Australian Author living in Country, Victoria. She is inspired by the world around her.

Read more at https://www.amazon.com/~/e/B0832T8F7Z.

9 798215 123188